TREE

A gentle story of love and loss

Lynn Jenkins

illustrated by

Kirrili Lonergan

EK

When your little one experiences a loss of any type, they experience big feelings — just like we do. We all need to have an idea about what to do with those big feelings.

In this latest Loppy and Curly story, Loppy experiences loss when his beloved friend, Tree, comes to the end of her life. Curly gently encourages Loppy to feel his big feelings and accept them, and then guides Loppy, together with the other LACs and Calmsters, to say goodbye in a way that will keep Tree fondly in their memories.

As your little ones go through their losses, Loppy and Curly will be with them the whole way. Knowing that Loppy is feeling how they might be will help your kids to feel like they have a little 'ally in loss'. Curly will be there too to softly give them ideas about what they can do to say goodbye and incorporate their loss into their lives.

We hope you enjoy this gentle story of love and loss, as you follow the red-and-white tail through *Tree's* pages.

Lynn and Kirrili

xx

Visit www.lessonsofalac.com to find out about the other books in the series:

Lessons of a LAC
Brave
Perfect Petunias
Grey-glasses-itis

As always to my children.
When you go through loss, may it be gentle x – L.J.

And just like that a bond was formed ...
for my dear JD – K.L.

In a little village at the very top of a mountain lived the Little Anxious Creatures (LACs) and the Calmsters. They all loved hanging out together, especially a LAC named Loppy and a Calmster named Curly.

One day, Loppy was studying
for a test and felt very worried.
So he went for a walk to visit
his old friend, Tree.

'What if I get all the
answers wrong?!'
Loppy wailed.

'What if I fail the test?!

Oh, Tree, I don't
know what to do!'

Whoosh …

whoosh …

whoosh …

The breeze blew through Tree's leaves,
and Loppy felt settled.

'Ah, Tree, I always feel better
when I'm near you.' Loppy laid his
head gently on Tree's long legs
stretching out over the ground.

'I get a Tree cuddle every time I
come here,' smiled Loppy.

Tree's tall, strong body stood
firm, and her long, wide arms
seemed to move with the breeze
to smile with Loppy.

Plop!

'Oh, my friend, you are losing your
leaves very quickly this year. Some of
your arms are almost bare!' said Curly.

'Let me tidy you up a bit.'

'It's a job to keep Tree tidy
these days isn't it, Curly?' said Loppy.

Curly looked up at Tree
and touched her trunk.

A sad look came over Curly's face.

'Tree's trunk is very dry and flaking. Have you noticed, Loppy, that Tree's leaves are falling off but it is not the time of year for them to fall?' said Curly.

'Well, yes,' replied Loppy. 'A whole heap just fell on my head!'

'I'm afraid our precious
friend is starting to
leave us, Loppy.'

'What! Oh no!

What will we do
without our Tree?

Tree can't go!'

'I know. The thought of Tree not being here anymore is very sad,' said Curly.

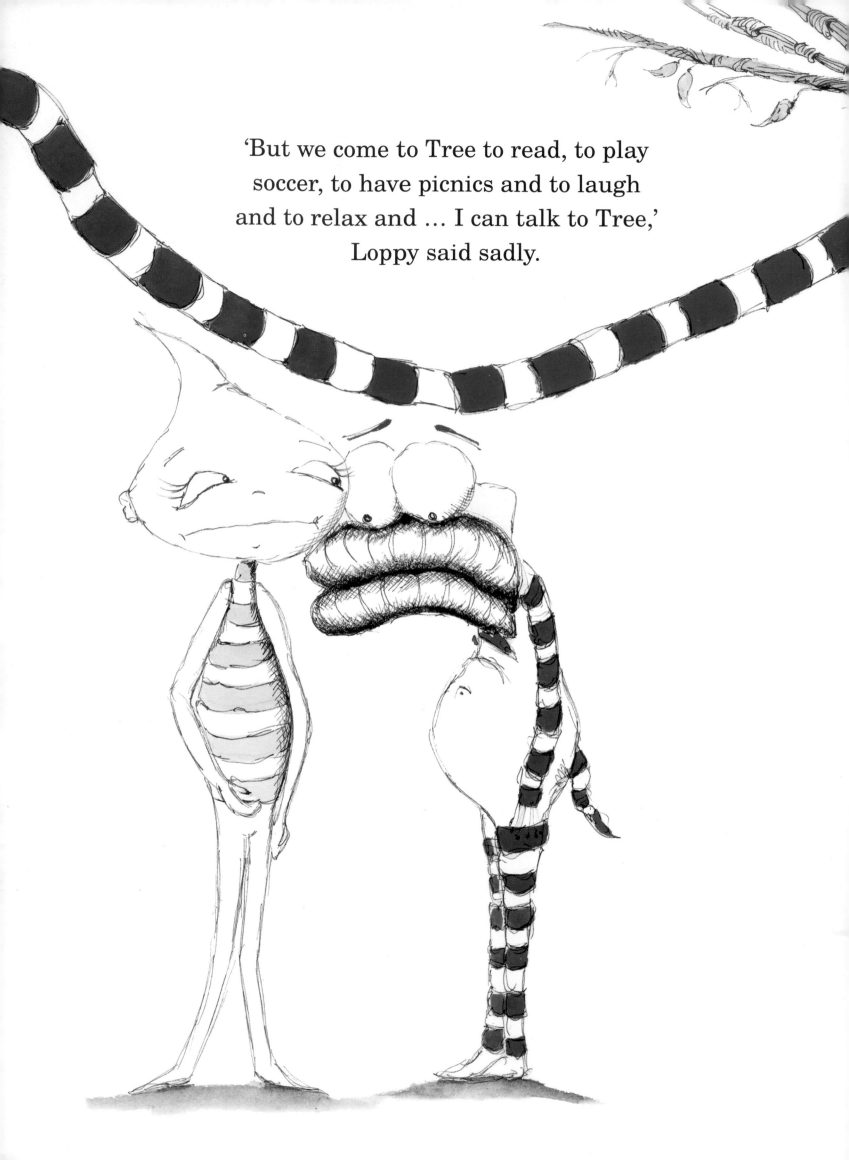

'But we come to Tree to read, to play
soccer, to have picnics and to laugh
and to relax and … I can talk to Tree,'
Loppy said sadly.

'I know, Loppy. Tree has stood in the centre of our village for a long, long time. But it is now Tree's time to go.'

Drop.

Drop.

Drop.

Loppy's tears fell at Tree's feet.

They gave Tree special presents.

They sat quietly with Tree and let Tree know what Tree meant to them.

They said goodbye to Tree …

A few months later, in the
centre of the village stood
a very special park.

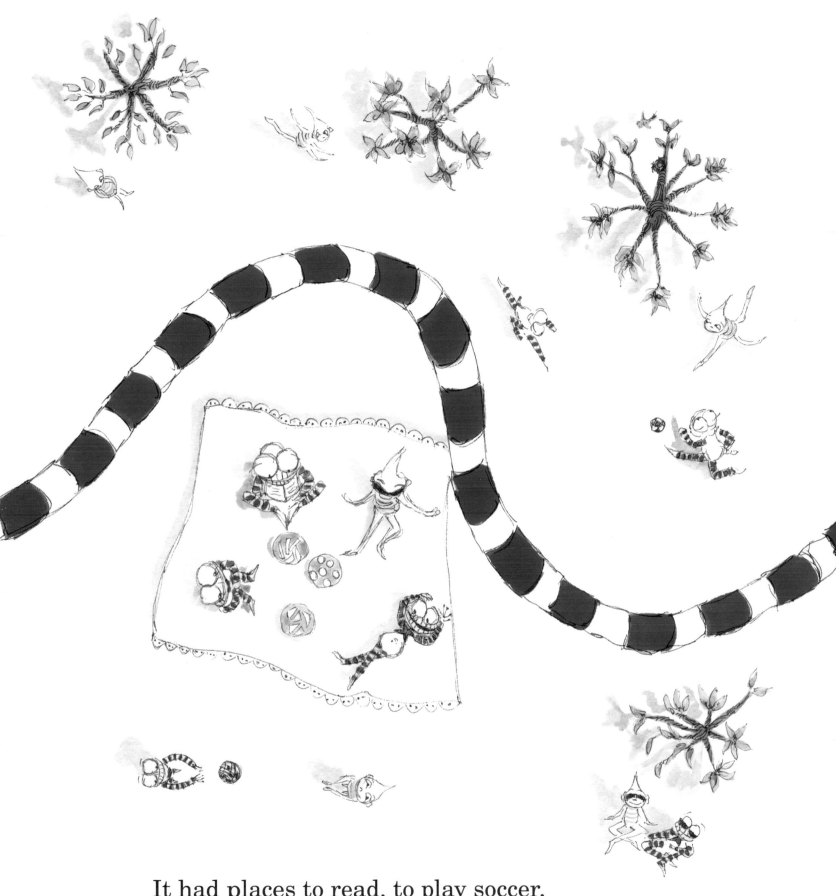

It had places to read, to play soccer,
to have picnics, to laugh and relax.
All the LACs and Calmsters were
having loads of fun.

On the very spot where Tree used to
stand, there was a very special chair
with a very special photo.

'This is for you, Tree,' said Loppy sitting on the
chair looking around the park. 'We will ALWAYS
remember just how special you were.'

'Especially to me,' Loppy smiled.

First published 2020

EK Books
an imprint of Exisle Publishing Pty Ltd
PO Box 864, Chatswood, NSW 2057, Australia
226 High Street, Dunedin, 9016, New Zealand
www.ekbooks.org

A CiP record for this book is available from the National Library of Australia.

ISBN 978-1-925820-12-6

Designed by Mark Thacker
Typeset in TeX Gyre Schola 18 on 29pt
Printed in China

This book uses paper sourced under ISO 14001 guidelines from
well-managed forests and other controlled sources.

2 4 6 8 10 9 7 5 3 1

Over the next few days all the LACs
and Calmsters visited Tree.

They read to Tree.

They hugged Tree.

They talked to Tree and laughed with Tree.